The Think-Ups

CLAIRE ALEXANDER

CANDLEWICK PRESS

It was raining.
Anna and Kiki
were stuck inside,
wondering what
to play.

"Snakes and ladders?"
suggested Anna.
"Boring!" said Kiki.

"Hide and seek?"
asked Anna.
"But I already know
all your hiding places,"
Kiki said with a sigh.

Then Kiki came up
with an idea.

"We could play
the Think-Ups!" she said.

"What are the Think-Ups?"
asked Anna.

"Well," said Kiki, "all you have to do is think up a Think-Up and it will appear!"

"Really?" said Anna, who was not
at all sure about that.

"Of course!" cried Kiki. "Watch!"
And she thought up a Think-Up.

And the Think-Up she thought up was . . .

A bunny!
No, not just one bunny,
but lots of bunnies!

"I'll be Kiki Flower Blossom the vet,
and you can be Bob, my helper!"

"But I don't want to be Bob,
your helper," said Anna.
"I want to think up a Think-Up of my own!"

So she thought up a Think-Up,
and the Think-Up she thought up was . . .

A moose!
Just one,
but a very large one!
"And you may call me
Anna Wild,
the fearless explorer,"
sang Anna.

Kiki was a bit annoyed.
"OK, Bob, it's my turn now!"

So Kiki thought up another Think-Up,
and the Think-Up she thought up was . . .

An octopus!

Not just one octopus, but lots and
lots of wriggling, giggling octopuses!
"Quick, Kiki!" cried Anna. "Let's take them all to the
living room!"

Anna then calmed
all the Think-Ups
down with a story.
And it was working . . .

until Kiki had a secret Think-Up,
     and the Think-Up she thought up was . . .

A koala!

Well, not just one koala,
but lots and lots and lots
of HUNGRY koalas!

"Oh, Kiki! What have you done?" cried Anna.

"Sorry, Bob!" said Kiki.

"And please stop calling me Bob!" said Anna.

Then the koalas
headed for the door . . .

"Oh no!" cried Anna.
"They've found . . .

the kitchen!"

"Kiki," yelled Anna, "your think-ups are TOTALLY out of control!"

"Well, Bob, your moose is the biggest, messiest Think-Up ever!" shouted Kiki.

"My one moose is not as messy as all your Think-Ups!
And for the last time, my name is Anna Wild, not Bob!"

"I'm sorry, Anna Wild," said Kiki.
That's when she had an idea.
"Don't worry—I'll make it all better."

And Kiki thought up
a Think-Up, and the Think-Up
she thought up was . . .

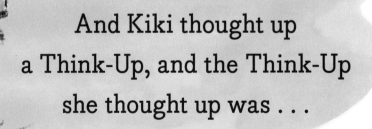

ALL

GONE!

"That was your best Think-Up yet,
Kiki Flower Blossom!"
Anna said with a smile.

Everything was back to normal,
and it had stopped raining.

"Let's go and play you-can't-catch-me
in the garden," said Kiki.
"Great idea," replied Anna.
"Just no more Think-Ups, okay?"

"Oh, Kiki!"
shrieked Anna.

But it was already too late . . .